LOS POSADAS

And bonus story

PANCHO CLAUS
VS. KRAMPUS

BY

V. CASTRO

CONTENTS

OTHER WORKS BY V. CASTRO

The Haunting of Alejandra

Immortal Pleasures

The Queen of The Cicadas

Mestiza Blood

Out of Aztlan

Hairspray and Switchblades

Dia de Los Slashers

Goddess of Filth

Rebel Moon

Alien: Vasquez

LOS POSADAS

V. Castro

*Dedicated to Santa Muerte, familia,
readers, reviewers, and all the fans.
Thank you.*

LOS POSADAS

I always said I would buy my mother a home. It would be just for her in those golden years without a husband. She had been through two bad divorces, single parenthood, and working through two degrees with two children. Now I could finally make good on the promise I'd made to myself that drove me to my success, even if it had bled me in the process.

We stood arm in arm outside the two-story, three-bedroom home in the town of New Braunfels. It's a wonderful little town in Texas between two very different cities. We were both born in San Antonio, a now sprawling city of Targets and freeways with The Alamo sitting at its heart. Austin is on the opposite side of New Braunfels. A little too vegan and hip for her with terrible traffic. Plus, people from California were moving there in droves.

She squeezed my arm tightly. Her voice cracked. "This is too much. I can't let you do this."

Tears streamed down my cheeks as I remembered all those years of hard work and fighting past doubt. And the years we had to live with family when we didn't have a home of our own. "I can and I already did. You deserve this."

It had been our way not to know in our hearts what we truly deserved, or were capable of. I held her close like a mother would a child. My tears continued to spill over cheek bones that possessed the same sharp angle as hers. Then a calm passed over me. Some dreams are real. I knew about nightmares and demons. This was the good stuff, the stuff of holiday movies and feel-good books. I chuckled as this reality hit me in full bloom.

"C'mon, Mom. Let's go check out your new home."

"*Our* home for a little bit. I'm glad you will be living with me."

I had one last surprise. As Christmas approached, I had taken the liberty of decorating the entire house for her after choosing simple furnishings she could change if she wanted. In the vast open plan living and dining room, I set up a seven foot tree with red, gold, and green glass baubles. White lights illuminated the two poinsettias on either side of the fireplace on the right side of the living room. It's Texas, so I wasn't sure how much use she would get out of it, but it was a nice cozy touch. Inside, I nestled fern-scented white pillar candles. On the mantle, I placed a series of nichos I'd purchased from small vendors in Market Square in San Antonio. Each little box depicted various saints. The last one was the birth of Christ in a manger. A tiny burro nestled close. I loved seeing La Virgen as La Catrina, her face a skull beneath blue robes as her pits for eyes gazed upon a baby Christ who also was just swaddled bones.

On the opposite left side wall, there was a credenza with a family altar I'd created. Instead of poinsettias I had two glass vases with blood red roses, one for us and the others for those passed. The roses brought the altar alive when the candles were lit. For years we remained apart as a family, each doing their own thing in their own way. People passed away. Babies were born. Marriages and divorces. I united us all, and our beliefs, on a red lace cloth with seven seven-day candles, a mini Christmas tree decorated with tiny red ribbons, family photos, and a crystal bowl filled with fruit as the offering next to a smaller ceramic bowl filled with holy water. A single stick of copal in a diffuser. There was a mix of her Christian ways and the beliefs I was becoming closer to with brujeria. The combination of the candles and incense smelled divine. I hoped this would be a new family home where we could all gather on the holidays, or just for the hell of it. She burst into fresh sobs on my shoulder as she scanned the interior. "I don't want to go on my cruise now! I want to stay here with you."

"Mom. You are going on that cruise with your sisters. You have never done that before. You all need to take some time to reconnect. Go live that *Golden Girls* dream. I'll be fine here. I've got my puzzle club. The gym. Probably do some baking. Have fun. You earned it."

She threw her arms around me and kissed me on the forehead before pulling away and making the sign of the cross in front of me. "You are protected!"

She dipped her fingers in the holy water and sprinkled it over the roses. "May these bring blessing, too!"

I fought the urge to roll my eyes because I didn't believe in God or Jesus the same way she did. That didn't matter now. Her love was protection enough.

"Thanks, mom. Now let me show you the rest of the house."

"My room have a big window? You know I like the fresh air when I sleep. I don't need anything else."

"Yes, you have the biggest room with a walk-in closet, bathroom, and big windows."

She wiped her mascara-stained cheeks. It felt so good to do this because she had never purchased a property for herself and she probably would never spend this kind of money on something she really wanted. Too extravagant. I, on the other hand, had no problem enjoying this new phase of life.

❦ ❦ ❦

We spent the rest of the evening listening to Christmas music and flipping through trashy magazines. I placed mine down when Jeff Buckley's version of "Hallelujah" began to play. The lights on the tree seemed to dim slightly as I thought about the possibility of spending another Christmas alone. My love life could be described as that single bulb on a string of Christmas lights that doesn't quite work and because of that it ruins the entire thing. My ability to find a healthy relationship up to this point had been as easy as unknotting that damn string of lights after it's been thrown in a box for a year. I decided to take love out of the equation so the rest of my life could flourish. And it did. Working on myself without distraction was the best Christmas gift I could ever give myself. But the desire for connection, deep connection, like the ghost of Christmas past, always shook chains in my heart. My soul knew there was real love out there to be experienced. As much as I tried to fight it, the need for intimacy and physical touch was a longing and need I couldn't deny. Whoever came next had to expect hours of lovemaking until we both resembled dried, over-cooked turkeys. Every bodily fluid drained until nothing was left. All we would want would be to chat lazily about how quickly the year went by, or moving aching muscles to order takeaway. That was my one and only wish I would make on Las Posadas when I lit the candles.

My mother and I went to bed at a modest 11 p.m. without the worry of a hangover. The last thought before I closed my eyes was seeing Henry the next day. He was the mortician and funeral director I could feel myself falling for. I wanted him the first time we met. If I had one wish, it would be to make love to him Christmas Eve into Christmas morning.

His occupation is what led me to him. I was doing research for a script with lengthy funeral scenes. The outline was due soon. The rest, as they say, is history.

I walked into the funeral home not knowing what to expect. I guess I pictured an older gentleman or couple who talked in hush tones while trying to sell you something you wish you didn't need. Maybe someone with a macabre fascination with death and no social skills. But those were stereotypes from the books and films I devoured in my youth. The website for the funeral home was still under construction, so no photos. I just hoped I could get the inspiration required to make the scenes as dramatic as possible.

How does one break out of a coffin? How long can you breathe in there? Does it smell?

A little bell rang when I entered. The heavy scent of floral candles burning blanketed the air. I brought my hand to my nose because there was something else clawing beneath jasmine and rose. Decay. Maybe that was normal? Other than that it was clean with no carpets. Hard wood floors gleamed with a freshly stained glow, and a range of coffins were on show like a sneaker display.

"I know. Sorry about that. I pulled out all the carpets trying to get that scent out of here. Plumbers, builders, all don't know what to tell me."

I turned to see a tall man wearing loose jeans and a red plaid shirt with the sleeves rolled up. He wore casual Adidas sneakers. His thick brown hair matched his eyes. I remained silent until I realised I was staring at him with an open mouth like some weirdo with no social skills.

"Oh, no problem. I don't care. I'm Nola. Hope it's okay I dropped by."

"I have no appointments, so you are in luck. The website is still being built. I bought this place from a couple who died. Their estate went to auction right at the time I wanted to stop working for local government and be my own boss. It's a great feeling."

I could feel myself smiling way too hard, like we were on a date. And he'd just told me the owners were dead. "That's great. I mean, not that they are dead, but you found something exciting. If you find it exciting , which I'm sure you do."

Fuck. That was why I couldn't get fucked. I toyed with my notebook like a shy school girl . . . in her forties.

He walked closer to me, his eyes meeting mine and his full lips in a thorn-like curve. "Nola, I'm Henry. How can I be of service?"

That question was loaded and it had nothing to do with funerals. He could service me bent over a coffin.

"I'm a writer, made-for-TV films, telenovela style. I have a character who locks another character in a coffin so she can steal her husband. But the wife escapes and there is a huge bust up."

He threw his head back. "Wow, now that is exciting."

"I just have a few questions. I'm happy to pay you for your time."

He shook his head. "How about a coffee sometime? I just moved here so I don't know the town."

My cheeks burned and so did my nipples. They could have been unlit candle wicks beneath the second-day hoodie I now regretted throwing on. Was he interested? "A coffee it is. I'll give you my number. Since I work from home I'm pretty flexible. And where from?"

"Dallas. I worked in the coroner's office. I work from home too. I like that. Well, why don't I make you a cup of coffee or tea and we can get started now? I'm all yours."

I licked my lips. "Great."

"Let's sit in the sun room in the kitchen and chat. The scent is not as bad there."

"Was there any information about the building? I've driven past, but thankfully never had to use the services."

"Hardly any information about the history was left for me. The couple died in a house fire. Not sure why they didn't live here, since there's a kitchen and two bedrooms. I've settled in nicely. It was assumed all the paperwork for the house burned with them, though. Nothing left. And no one came forward after their deaths."

Despite not feeling cold, a shiver made me want to rub my arms. "Wow. That in itself makes a story. Wonder what this place could tell us. It looks pretty old, like the other historic buildings around here."

His body slightly jerked. Did he feel it too? "Want to see the rest of the place? It's still a work in progress . . . But only if you have time."

The more I could get to know him, the better. "I'm all yours."

He gave me a wide grin. Our eyes met again. "This way. Obviously this is the main area. The only work I did here was to the floors. Hardwood through the entire place, except where the bodies are prepared. It was so cheap I had money to spare to spruce up the place."

We moved through the large front display room and entered a parlor to the right. The arrangement room appeared darker than the display room from the overcast morning and large bushes that grew almost above the four windows. Lonely hooks hung on a rod above them.

"No curtains yet. I'm not into design, but the others were old and hideous. Someone is coming next week to replace them. And a company to cut those shrubs blocking all the light. They surround the entire house, but these are the only ones that cause any issues."

I didn't like it there. It made me think of my mother instead of romance with this attractive man. She was getting older, as was I. At the very front stood a single wreath of wilted red roses. Their once-lovely blossoms hung in sorrow, their life over. They had nothing left to give except maybe decoration in a potpourri bowl. Not the same as fresh flowers, or even better an entire garden that sprouted year round. God, I was happy to have bought a property and be looking for another for myself. Giving my mother a place she could age in comfort without any worries was something I would never regret. It was a fresh start. Maybe this chance meeting was one as well.

"This is the room I like to spend time in the least. I always remember the last person laid out here and their families mourning." I turned and touched his forearm instinctively. He was impossibly beautiful to me. And interesting. "Show me the rest," I said.

We moved to an adjacent room to the left which was an office. There were two identical, simple, antique, dark wood desks that stood on ornately carved furry legs and hooves. One remained empty, while the other had a large, expensive looking monitor and keyboard. There were Bose speakers I doubted the previous owners had purchased.

"I know what you're thinking. Strange desks, but I couldn't get rid of them. Plus, you never know what the future holds. Might need it one day, and they obviously go together."

My fingertips traced the wood of the empty desk waiting for a companion. The feeling of the surface made me think the previous owners took good care of them. There were no drink rings or scratched spots. It was regularly stained and oiled. "I like them. They're . . . unique."

He stepped closer to me as if he wanted to touch my back, but then hesitated. His hands went into his pockets instead. Damn. I appreciated him being a gentleman instead of a creep. As a woman, I had to fend off many of them, although this was one I would gladly give an invitation. I hoped at some point it could happen. Please, La Virgen, let him be single and into females.

He led me through another open door on the left side of the office that had a short landing before descending to the basement. "If you don't feel comfortable down here, we can run back up. This is where the bodies are prepared. There is also another part of the basement I will show you, but we don't have to go in. Even I hate it. Part of me thinks the smell is coming from there. But when I brought in an architect to see what we could do with it he said nothing substantial because it would compromise the entire home. That was only the second time I went all the way in there. I tried to chip away at the walls with no luck before he arrived. I didn't get far before I had to stop. My body shivered like never before. Didn't bother to look through the soggy boxes left before having them removed from the room. When they were placed on the lawn in the

23

open air and daylight I tried to look through them. Everything was ruined with mold, and indecipherable. They went to the dump. There were also three rotting coffins. Must have been from when the previous owners first started. All of it gone."

The way he spoke of the room frightened me. "What about where the bodies go?"

"That place is fine. I put on my music and nothing can distract me."

At the bottom of the stairs was a small hallway and two doors. One was shut and the other open with the light on. He was right. The preparation room appeared sterile and bright. It wasn't new, but had been kept in good condition. Nothing seemed out of place.

"Now the other?"

He looked at me with what could have been a slice of fear. "You sure? I'll open the door and shine the flashlight. The main light has a pull cord in the center of the room. I'd rather not."

My mom would love him. She was into her superstitions. "Really? That bad?"

He opened the unlocked door and bent over to pick up the large flashlight. It was a horrible room. The concrete floor appeared tiled with square stains of mold where the removed boxes had been. There were also damp spots from water that didn't come from anywhere obvious. The walls were cobbled stones stacked tightly together. In the light they seemed wet with a light, slimy sheen. A seam of removed grout bolted down the right-hand wall. The aroma of decay clung in the air stronger than the other rooms.

"You think this could be the source of the smell?"

"Yes. Those stones won't budge and the architect said I couldn't just blast through. I wish I knew who built it."

"Sounds like a horror story, and a big jigsaw that will never be put together."

He turned to me with a wide, boyish grin. "You like puzzles?"

"I don't dislike them, just been on the grind with work for a few years. Things are easing up now."

"Hey, I know it sounds dorky especially since I also dislike dark basements, but . . . I have a thing for them?"

I had never had strong feeling about puzzles, but it sounded fun. And he would be there. Doing puzzles while getting to know each other was much better than fucking him after a few cocktails at a bar with such fury it would scare him off.

"Puzzles are great. All my friends are married with kids and fight over who gets to go out until no one does. I'm in."

"I know what you mean, single life . . ."

Inside I was SCREAMING. We were both available. "Great."

"Puzzle Club, it's called. We meet up with beer or wine, bring a dish, then put together a jigsaw."

My heart raced and my nipples wanted to fly into his mouth. Before I could respond, we both whipped our heads towards the open dark room. In my peripheral vision I thought I caught something moving in the light of the downcast flashlight. He must have seen it too because he brought the light back up to the empty room. The ray of brightness sliced through the dark in sharp cuts. Nothing there. I turned to step inside. One of my feet crossed the threshold. It felt cold, but no wonder with the concrete floor and stone cobbled walls. He touched my forearm before I could go further inside. "Let's go back upstairs. You have questions for me."

He was right. That room was not for entering. I hoped nothing ever exited either. My mom would have probably doused it in holy water and lined it with statues of La Virgen.

Puzzle Club was surprisingly better than expected. Everything about Henry was torn from all the stories I hoped would be my own until I remembered I lived in reality and not the worlds I created for a living or the books I read. He was the dream I sold to other people on screen. It beat staying at home with a bottle of wine in front of the TV getting drunk enough to text all the wrong people or sob over a meal for one. But a meal for one is infinitely nicer than a meal with the wrong one. The one who said I couldn't do it. Shouldn't do it. Asked, *what is wrong with you*? Don't look like that. Don't write like that. Just be small for me. No thanks. Hard work and divine timing selling my over-the-top scripts enabled me to buy my mother a home.

At Puzzle Club I met Carlos and Robin, both people I would not have met otherwise. They were my small puzzle crew. Robin was a kindergarten teacher. Carlos was retired military filling his days with dog walking, books and jigsaws. And then there was Henry, the sexiest and kindest funeral director I had ever met. It didn't bother me at all he messed with dead bodies, not when he looked at me across the table during Puzzle Club when trying to figure out what piece to put where. For weeks we brushed against each other when serving ourselves food. Fingertips reaching for the same pieces. Our eyes meeting across the table. I feasted on his presence. After six Puzzle Clubs filled with agonizing silent lust, and at the one just before my turn to host for Christmas, it finally happened.

It was Henry's turn to host. Robin and Carlos left, but I stayed behind to show Henry what all my questions for him had created. He wanted to read the outline for the drama I was writing.

"So . . . Night cap? I have rum or Baileys."

I stood next to him in the kitchen. "Since it's almost Christmas, how about a Baileys."

He poured two Baileys on ice for us. "You can have anything you want. Just ask."

I took the low-ball glass in my hand and lifted it to him. "Thank you. For inviting me to do puzzles and helping me with this research."

He lifted his glass to me. "Thank you for saying yes and making this new venture of mine . . . so worth it."

We clinked glasses. The thick creamy alcohol tasted sweet on my lips and washed down my throat with ease. I wanted to taste him like that Baileys, wanted his sweetness to fill my mouth before swallowing every drop as he shuddered in my arms.

I put the glass down and pressed my body to his. "This is me asking and giving you a free invitation."

Henry put his glass on the counter and wrapped both arms around my waist. "I accept."

His mouth tasted like mine, buttery richness. The longer we kissed the harder his cock pressed against my thigh. That night I wore a green v-neck sweater dress. My boots left at the front door. No bra or panties. Some women dream and hope, but never do. I always took the risks to turn fantasy into reality. And there we were.

I pulled away with his hand in mine. The kitchen was connected to the display room. I guided him to the closed coffin on the opposite side closest to the parlor.

"Here."

He chuckled, his hands on my waist, ready to explore my body. "Really? Is that your fantasy?"

I leaned against the coffin. It was slicker and a little more slippery than I'd thought it would be. His touch was gentle yet firm when gripping the pliable flesh of my thick ass. With a gentle touch, he massaged my hips, "Your curves . . . the softness and warmth you always bring when I see you."

My lips dug into his neck as I gave every kiss I had wanted to give him since we met. His fingers slipped between my legs. I let out a small moan as I was already fully aroused. His eyes glinted in the light of the scented candles in the room. My thighs felt sticky and damp as his fingers explored me completely. Being this close scared every demon out of me. All my starved insecurities broke free from the dungeons where I kept my past hurts, all those plans and hopes dashed when someone chose not to stay. But I wanted to give love one more chance. If my miracle was to manifest, it would be during Las Posadas.

I didn't want his lips and hands to stop searching me, putting me back together again after being emotionally and mentally scattered for so long.

Our mouths met with more hunger than I imagined he possessed. My fingers fumbled with his jeans before touching him the way he touched me. Every stroke brought him more to life. I couldn't wait any longer. I turned around because I feared falling backwards if I sat on the curved coffin top. This wasn't a romcom. I needed to be satisfied and to satisfy him in return.

I lifted my sweater dress. Both his hands circled the entire width of my hips and ass. I placed one foot on the platform the coffin rested on. My forehead touched the cold object as he entered me. A perfect fit. His first and second thrusts made me bite my lip as the ease of our fucking already felt orgasm-inducing. My breath fogged the polished wood with a prayer of ecstasy and pure pleasure, both of my palms splayed on the smooth surface. He thrust at a smooth, rhythmic pace from slow to fast, never leaving a single inch of his cock from dipping into what felt like an untapped reservoir like the ones beneath the vast state of Texas. I could feel my clit getting closer to releasing all the tension of our unspoken wants and needs.

And then Henry shouted without warning, "The fuck?"

I looked up and screamed. From across the parlor I could see a silhouette peeking into one of the windows. My arms crossed my breasts.

"Shit! Maybe I should have left those bushes until I got the new curtains!" Henry ran to the window and looked side to side. "I'm sorry about that. I didn't think anyone would be prowling around here."

In the porch light shining through the window I admired his body. His presence alone aroused me. My fright had subsided and I didn't really care if someone watched. He turned and walked back towards me.

"You don't want to get dressed? Are you scared?"

I dropped my arms. "No. Not scared and not getting dressed. I didn't come yet."

He stood before me with one hand on my ass. "Then what scares you?"

I touched his chest feeling my own squeeze with emotion, my vulnerability melting me from inside. "Another heartbreak."

The back of his left hand caressed my cheek. "I'm not in the business of breaking hearts, and yours is certainly one I do not want hurting because of me. I don't do casual. I see death all the time, but I also see the love people can possess for another. Playing around gets old and life is short."

"Why don't we go to your bed? I haven't seen that part of the house yet. Show me what else you can do."

He brushed my long hair from my face and breasts. "How about I figure you out like a puzzle. I want to know where every piece fits and the detail of each one."

"Deal."

⚜ ⚜ ⚜

I woke up on the first day of Las Posadas wanting Henry. It was still dark when I saw my mother off for her trip on the day we usually spent together.

"You sure you will be alright? It's Las Posadas. I don't like the idea of us not celebrating together. Why didn't you come with us?"

"Yes, Mom! Get in that taxi and enjoy the sun. Mexico is perfect this time of year. And you know I have to finish this script. I would be too distracted there."

"Mija, I will tell you this one thing. I know you are going out; you never know when someone will be unexpectedly brought into your life. The right one won't leave you for anything. They will see your worth and value without question."

"I know. It will happen. Maybe sooner than I think."

Her love-filled smile turned a frown. She looked upstairs. "Wait, I left my window open."

"Go! I'll deal with it."

We kissed on the cheek, and then I watched her rush off with her wheely bag for a much needed vacation with her sisters who worked just as hard as she did. I come from a long line of incredible women. They are the women no one notices in life despite them being shining stars in their own way. Gems hidden beneath soil.

With my mother out the door, I had to get started on my dishes for the Las Posadas Puzzle Club I was hosting. Just past 7 a.m., I had all day, and it was a good day with fond memories. Las Posadas. It's what true Christmas spirit is about with family coming together. The story celebrates Mary and Joseph being welcomed inside for the birth of Jesus after an arduous journey. I even bought a small seven pointed star piñata to remind me of that struggle I waged with myself and the struggles of my mother from her upbringing. The piñata signifies the seven deadly sins that always find their way to self-sabotage. I had indulged in all of them at one point in my life. A few times all in one night. The piñata stick I rested next to my altar. The stick represents faith and love. I never went to church, despised it really, but I believed in something. I liked Brujeria. It felt right. Perhaps a stick in my dining room was as good as anything else I could believe in. It could always be used on an intruder.

☙ ☙ ☙

With the sun down and minutes to spare, I was ready to welcome my friends into my home. Which also meant welcoming Henry into my home. He hadn't been to my old apartment before I moved; I always went to the funeral home or the Puzzle Club locations. If I were my younger self, I would be wearing the tiniest dress I could find and the reddest of lipsticks with nothing but seduction on my mind (although seduction was always on my mind). With Henry, though, I wanted to be the real me without the fuss of trying to be sexy. I liked how I looked, but I needed something deeper. I went for a *Gremlins* Christmas sweater—the kind they say are ugly, but damn if Gizmo isn't always cute. It has been my favorite Christmas movie since I could remember. Every year I watched *Gremlins* and *A Muppet Christmas* with my mother.

The doorbell rang just as I placed the second pot of tamales on the table. A pot of pozole simmered on low in the kitchen with bowls of it already on the table. I ran to the laundry room at the far end of the kitchen to open the window to allow the kitchen heat to dissipate. The small window above the sink in the kitchen already open. If I was alone, I would have never opened the windows, but I wasn't and this was the Gruene historic district. Sleepy and safe. I opened the door in time as the second bell rang.

Robin stood there with Henry and Carlos just behind.

"This place is beautiful." Robin swivelled her head around admiring the décor as she stepped inside.

"Thank you. I bought it for my mom. I'm living here while I look for a permanent place for myself. Tired of paying rent on a one bedroom with a view of nothing."

Henry held up a box in one hand and a bag from Whole Foods in the other. Not the prettiest box I had seen, but it made my stomach flutter like falling snow in a breeze. You don't notice the cold when snow is that beautiful. "Just place it on the sofa. Thank you." Before walking past me, his lips curled to a smile. "Now that is a fantastic sweater." Carlos gave me a one-armed hug followed by a kiss on the cheek as he entered. "What was that?" His eyes darted side to side.

I looked around. "Huh? I didn't hear anything."

Then I remembered. "There is an open window upstairs. Probably the wind."

He tore his eyes from the ceiling. "Oh. I'm getting old. I spent too much time on high alert in the military. Wouldn't know it now." He patted his belly that was hardly there.

Henry and Robin were already seated at the dining table behind the sofa when Carlos and I joined them. "Last Christmas" by Wham played softly as I set the table. "Oooh, smells wonderful! What do you have?" Robin's eyes devoured the dishes I prepared. She always seemed perpetually chirpy with a high ponytail and big smile.

Henry stood across from me scanning the spread. "Can I help you do anything else? This looks amazing. It puts mine last week to shame."

I couldn't help stifling a little giggle thinking about our coffin sex. "I think you did an amazing job."

He looked into my eyes and then away again as he blushed.

Robin and Carlos dug into the food and bopped to the music. Henry looked quizzically at a steaming bowl of pozole before taking a mouthful. I pinched myself mentally for wanting him to like it. He swallowed, glanced at me before diving in. "This is great."

"And vegetarian," I said too eagerly.

"Mexican food without meat?" asked Carlos.

I rolled my eyes at Carlos. "Yes. And the beans in the bean and cheese tamales don't have lard either. You sound like my mom, Carlos." He shrugged his shoulders and grabbed one bean and cheese with two other pork tamales. "Yeah, my doctor says I need to cut out the saturated fat. But it tastes so damn good. And you sound like my daughter who lives in Austin. Quinoa this and quinoa that is all I hear." Carlos unwrapped his tamales like a child on Christmas morning. His delight in that first bite put a smile on my face. When I wasn't creating telenovelas, I enjoyed feeding people. Both warmed my soul.

Henry put his spoon down. "I got something interesting left at my door."

We all stopped piling our plates with food. Puzzle Club was hardly interesting, or well-known. Robin had pinned a few cards in a couple of grocery store noticeboards, coffee shops, and church halls. Because Henry had a formal business, all inquiries were directed there. I doubted whatever was left would set the night on fire.

"What is it?" Robin asked as she sat down with her plate.

Henry flicked his head towards the sofa. "The wrapped box I gave to Nola."

I felt heat on my cheeks. I'd thought it was a gift for me. Suddenly, I felt foolish even entertaining the idea that he thought of me half as much as I silently thought of him.

Carlos stopped his lip smacking. "Why don't we finish the meal, then get started? I brought a killer puzzle from Hallmark I found at Goodwill. It's textured, too. Cats playing under a Christmas tree. When we are done, I will give it to my granddaughter. They don't make many like that anymore."

Christmas music filled the room, as did our usual casual conversation about life, the greatest puzzle of them all—aside from love. I tried not to look over at Henry too much to give him the wrong impression. Boy, did I master the art of coming on too strong. Perhaps that is why my telenovela made-for-TV movies got picked up. Nothing held back in the story, a tidal wave of emotion and action. Love lost and found with drama to leave you hanging off your seat. People love watching the torment of tension and the release when it breaks, like sex. Now I took pride in being subdued in my day-to-day life. Brujeria grounded me in the earth where I would return to be with my ancestors. Not fighting the creatures of the night inside of me, or the ones who wanted to own me. For me, Las Posadas went from a Catholic thing as a kid to a worship of the ancestors and the possibility that the spirits they worshipped could be real. If we were not alone here on this rock in a one-dimensional plane, what else was there?

When no one could shove another thing in their mouth, I moved us to the glass coffee table I had cleared for the puzzle. Henry stood close to me, his eyes darting to Carlos and Robin as they topped up their drinks.

"Can I talk to you about something?"

My heart pinched. Was he about to friend zone me in a neutral safe place amongst friends? He got what he wanted and that was it? Just when you think you have healed those past hurts, they like to rear their monstrous anxious heads again. Dripping your mind and heart in bloody spit. The past likes to make a meal of you every once in awhile even when you think you have left it somewhere buried to never hurt you again.

"Sure. Come with me to start the dishwasher." My heart thumped with every footstep. The cool breeze from the open window felt good.

"That box I brought. It was for the club. Not for you."

"I know." I didn't want to embarrass myself by showing him my emotions and fiddled with the dishwasher buttons.

"Well, I have something just for you. It's at my place. If you don't have plans on Christmas . . . maybe we can open it together."

I paused deliberately because I might have thrown him to the ground and ridden him like a sleigh after what he did to my body all night and into the morning. Then he'd brought me coffee and a store-bought cranberry muffin in bed. My worst fears were just that. Candle smoke. Sure, I could be alone, but that wasn't how I wanted my story to end. I hadn't bought anything for him yet because I had this bad habit of over-giving. If I saw something someone I knew would enjoy, it was an instinct to get it for them. How many times in life were we gifted without anything expected in return.

"I would love that. And thank you."

"Okay, you two. Let's do this!" belted Carlos over the music and dishwasher sounds.

As we walked back to the others, Henry's fingertips touched my lower back just beneath the bottom of my sweater and at the waist of my leggings, causing my flesh to pucker in arousal. I wanted to feel his hand cupping my ass. It reminded me how he gently guided my hips as we made love on the coffin before being interrupted. I swiped a handful of napkins for the coffee table in the event of a spilled drink.

The unwrapped box sat in the middle of the coffee table and we all stared at it without moving. A folded square of the wrapping paper was taped to the front of the box. In black marker it said, *A Puzzle*. "Who is going to do the honors?" Carlos asked.

Henry met my eyes as we sat on the floor. "Nola is the host. She can be the one." I smiled before sliding the box in front of me. The paper appeared old fashioned. Maybe reused, with all the white creases covering it. The tape appeared yellowed and ripped, not cut with scissors. The print was of different types of birds with a snowy background. They were woodland birds including crows.

Something inside shuffled when I ripped the paper. Puzzle pieces? The burning fern tree candles smelled stronger, the air thicker. Everyone looked on with curious expectation.

"Whoa. That is a strange one." Robin pulled away from the table as she said this.

I lifted the simple cardboard box and twisted it every which way to find out where it originated. No barcode. No toy company logo. Nothing that could identify where it was from. The picture that appeared hand-painted on the front could only be described as hideous. In the center of the image was an old crone. Her clothing was haggard, filthy. The scarf tied around her head and beneath the chin looked speckled with blood. One of her feet peeked from under her skirts. It was webbed with thick claws curled into the ground. She held a basket filled with wailing cherubic children. A dead body hung from the rafter of a hut. A jagged seam of leather thread from pubis to neck held in tufts of straw which were poking through. Bowels and organs spilled onto the floor beneath the body. The grin on her face relished the slaughter. The pupils were a mere single dot of black. Hideous.

"May I have a look?"

I handed Henry the box. He adjusted his glasses. Henry had that Indiana Jones thing going on when he concentrated hard on a puzzle. He only wore glasses with puzzles or reading. His mouth and jaw tensed and released as he searched. His cheeks slightly flushed as we neared the end. Many times, I wrote a text to him about something random and then immediately deleted it. I shook off these thoughts.

He adjusted himself on the floor. "This reminds me of an old folktale. You ever hear of Perchta?"

"Who?" Carlos scrunched his nose.

"The Perchta witch. My family is from Austria. Hence the name, Gruene. This area was settled by German immigrants. Maybe someone had this in their family and handed it down. Basically, she stalks people who are not doing as they are told, children and adults. She disembowels them and then stuffs their bodies with garbage and straw."

"Well good thing we have our own bruja, too. And it is Las Posadas. I like to think we are protected." Carlos looked at me and then the altar I had set up.

"It's ugly; I'd prefer puppies in Santa hats, but I will give it a go. Plus, the cake Carlos brought smells amazing," said Robin.

Henry opened the box, which possessed another surprise. The pieces were made from wood. Perfectly shaped with smooth grooves and edges. The paint did not appear old or chipped. Whoever created this had to be a master craftsman.

"This is gonna be so hard. I can't wait! Next to Christmas, I love Halloween." Carlos let out a belly laugh and began to sort through the pieces. One side had the image, but the other side something else. Black markings. I wondered if it was a double-sided puzzle. Everything about it felt deliberate.

As we worked our way through the puzzle, I could feel that little niggle of longing again. Each of the pieces different in shape, part of this bigger picture. But not all fit together. A piece locked perfectly with another. Made for that shape. They shared a small corner harmoniously. So many nights I looked to my left wanting someone to read my script. Laugh at it, cry with me. A squeeze on the thigh, hugs when times were low. Just a piece that understood what my edges needed. I glanced towards Henry. *Maybe*.

"Shit. I'm so sorry Nola, I cracked one." Robin had knocked over a glass bauble from the tree as she returned to the coffee table after refreshing her eggnog.

"No problem. I'll get rid of it." I scooped the bauble from the carpet. A piece broke off in my hand. The pain ripped through my fingers. "Fuck!" I moved my hand to the coffee table to avoid getting blood on the new cream carpet. Henry immediately placed his hand beneath mine. "Fuck!" he shouted. A shard pierced his palm. His hand held mine as our blood comingled and dripped on the puzzle.

"That's really weird." Robin stared at the puzzle with her hand midair holding a Santa head-shaped napkin. We looked at the puzzle. The blood no longer remained on the surface. It was as if the wood drank it all. Henry removed his hand from mine. He passed me a napkin before grabbing one for himself from the coffee table. With his left thumb applying pressure to the cut, he picked up one of the pieces, holding it up to the light of the chandelier above the dining table. His fingers ran across the piece.

"This wood . . . it makes me think . . . it reminds me of something I found when I moved here. But that is ridiculous. Let's finish this weird thing."

Under any other circumstances, I would have skipped the puzzle and gone for the one Carlos brought. But I needed to see what was on the other side. "Yes, we should. Did you guys notice the back of the pieces? Black marks. I think it might be double-sided."

The other three looked at me in silence before putting their heads down to work faster. I cleaned my hand and wrapped the broken bauble in the napkin. The cuts were only superficial. It didn't take long for the picture on the puzzle to match the box as the flurry of hands placed each piece.

Not caring what they might think, I craned my neck beneath the table to see what was on the underside. My heart rate spiked, the eggnog threatening to spew from my mouth. First the frightening puzzle and now this message. I took my phone from my pocket and snapped a photo. I shimmied back up and held out my phone. Robin brought her hand to her mouth. The underside of the puzzle read, *First the fear then the feast. I will bleed the world dry.*

Henry's eyes widened. "When I bought the funeral home there was a coffin in the basement. It smelled rancid. We brought it out to the lawn with the rest of the junk in the basement. This was inscribed on the inside. It scared the shit out of me. I thought maybe it was a prop for Halloween made from something they had to spare, but that explanation seemed odd. Why would an old couple do that?"

Robin's body shook like someone had breathed on her neck. "I think I need to use the bathroom."

"It's just through the kitchen. Hang a left and it's right next to the laundry room."

"Thanks."

As she walked away, I called out, "Do you mind bringing back Band-Aids from the medicine cabinet?"

"Sure thing."

Henry, Carlos, and I continued to stare at the strange puzzle, trying to put together all the pieces of the evening. "So what did you do with the coffin?" asked Carlos.

"I chopped it up according to green waste recycling rules and left it on the curb for collection. Next morning the pile was gone."

"I know you had very little paper trace on the previous owners, but did you talk to anyone about them?" My storyteller mind worked fast. Sometimes it worked faster than I could write, the emotion and images pulling me with undertow rage.

"From what the people who dealt with them told me, they were almost like zombies. It got worse year after year. Kept to themselves. Nice enough. No one who knew them from when they first started the business was around . . . and by that I mean alive."

My hand throbbed. My eyes caught the single candle I lit on my altar. The smoke trailed into the atmosphere as a black pillar. The glass was completely black with soot. Something was not right. I wondered how long Robin had been gone. I wasn't the only one to think it. Carlos rose from the sofa. "I want to check on Robin. She seemed a little disturbed. Maybe too much eggnog."

I nodded and turned back to Henry. Despite my fear, it was terribly romantic with the decorations and my family photos in the background to give us a blessing. I hoped for a fresh start. We both opened our mouths to speak when we heard a scream that possessed the power to break the outdoor Christmas lights of an entire neighborhood.

Henry and I leapt to our feet and ran towards the bathroom. Carlos stood outside the doorway of the laundry room. Robin lay on the floor, her neck torn in a wide gash. Another body, a stranger, hung from a noose attached to the laundry room light. Her bowels were strung across the cabinets, washer, and dryer like string of red tinsel. Blood streaked the walls, some forming candy cane arcs. Carlos heaved and vomited on Henry's shoes. The stench of garbage emanated from the hanging body. It was no wonder because she was slit from belly button to neck. Her skin bulged as if she had been stuffed. It appeared she had. Straw and garbage poked through the misshapen seams of her vertical wound.

"There is a killer in this house! Call the police! My phone doesn't have any battery," screamed Carlos as he looked up at me with bean and cheese hanging from his lips. His eyes glistened with tears.

Henry patted his pockets. "I left mine in the car. I don't like distractions during Puzzle Club."

"My phone is on the sofa," I said, looking at Henry.

There was a bump above our heads followed by heavy footfalls. Carlos looked around. "Now I know that ain't Santa. Do you have any weapons in this house?"

I shook my head. "My knife block in the kitchen?"

He bounded towards the kitchen with Henry and I in tow. The footfalls had stopped and now we knew why. A creature appearing half man and half something else entirely crouched on my dining table. He wore a tattered tuxedo that hung off his thin frame. His greasy brown hair parted down the center just past his angular cheeks. His eyes were as red as the blood that covered his mouth.

"Don't come any closer, cabrón!" Carlos shouted as he grabbed the largest knife from the wood block, pointing it towards the man who I could only think of as a vampire. His teeth were sharp splinters, dripping in what was most probably Robin's blood. "And what will you do, old man?" He rose to his full height, placing bloody fingernails with the same sharpness as his teeth on the ceiling, dragging them and leaving red icicles in the plaster. He began to kick the dishes off the table as he walked towards us. Food flew into the air. The three of us backed towards the kitchen.

Carlos looked in my direction past Henry. "Stay behind us, Nola. I'm still strong for a viejito."

"No chance, Carlos. I just bought this fucking house!"

The vampire turned his attention to me as he jumped from the table. "Aren't you pretty. Bet you taste just as good with all those spices in your blood. I love your sweater." His voice sounded soft, sultry. I half expected him to sound like a growling animal.

"What do you want?" I side-stepped closer to my altar on the credenza. I took the pinata stick in one hand. In my periphery were the red roses. I remembered my mother's blessing.

He looked at Henry. "Well, for starters, this one here destroyed my bed when he took over my caretakers' business after they ran out of usefulness. So, I would kill you, but I will make slaves of you two instead. My new caretakers, since I know how much you like each other. The house smelled like sex for days. You will craft another resting place for me, bring me victims, and do everything and anything I want. Humans are small. Be small for me."

The harmony I created for myself to be a better human began to vibrate inside. I had spent a fortune on therapy, I meditated. I'd climbed a mountain in

Africa for an entire week. Cried and prayed over my many mistakes, lies I told myself and others. I continued to try to master my emotions, my lust. My deep insecurities. The snow globe in which I had captured my blizzard of pain didn't just crack in that moment, it crashed onto the floor. I looked at the vampire. This creature came to torment and consume. It took pleasure in this. Why else create a puzzle? I could see it in its eyes. No way would I allow it to take this home or make me a half-alive zombie of a human. I did that for years. He wouldn't take away the world I'd built from scratch for myself. Take the life of my friend. The man I loved. Not on fucking Las Posadas. He would not fuck up me and my wish come true to make love to Henry all Christmas Eve and Christmas morning until we wanted to die.

The vampire lifted an elongated finger and rotated it between the three of us. "Now which one will be first? We could play spin the bottle. I know *you two* would love that." The vampire gave Henry and I a vicious grin, licking his lips, enjoying seeing us as what he perceived to be helpless.

From my periphery I could see something else. The small bowl with a painted image of La Virgen de Guadalupe filled with holy water. No vampire would suck the life out of me. Too many times had I submitted myself, and for what?

"Hey, cabrón."

The vampire looked at my direction. With my left hand I tossed the bowl of holy water in the vampire's face. He let out a guttural howl not of this earth, clawing at his eyes and neck.

"Henry! Grab the roses! Carlos! The pozole! I put extra garlic in there and it's still hot!" Carlos whipped himself around towards the kitchen, letting go of the knife and grabbing the pot. As the vampire recovered, Carlos tossed the still-hot pot over him. More wails from the vampire as he doubled over. His body contorted and spasmed. His flesh bubbled and popped. His nails grew with the shrieks of his pain.

"How much garlic is in there?" shouted Carlos.

"A lot. I'm Mexican!"

"Maybe I will kill you all instead," the vampire shrieked before grabbing Carlos by his arms and tossing him overhead into the Christmas tree. Carlos and the tree crashed to the ground. His body hit the remote control for the stereo, blasting music louder throughout the house. The fucking Bee Gees, "Stayin Alive." "Christ, Mom!" I shouted without thinking.

Henry glanced in my direction. "Your mom likes the Bee Gees too?"

The vampire looked disgusted with us. "How fitting that I take you now. Sappy humans stuck on sentiment. Listening to you between the walls has been like watching some god-awful show."

Henry slapped him across the face with the roses sprinkled with holy water. The vampire screamed again, wiping his eyes. He swiped Henry across the face with his viscera-caked nails, knocking him down. The vampire swivelled back to me at just the right time. Divine timing.

With the piñata stick firmly in one hand, I drove it through the heart of the vampire with all the strength in my 4'11 frame. He screeched as he thrashed around before collapsing on the floor. His eyes and ears oozed blood and some other viscous black fluid. I took the stick out of his chest and punctured him again. Both of his hands grabbed it tightly. His eyes filled with animosity. Henry crawled towards the vampire with the large knife Carlos dropped. "We finish it together."

I kneeled next to Henry. Both our hands held the knife as we sawed through flesh and muscle of the vampire's neck until we hit bone. I stood again, walked to my altar with the heavy crystal bowl. I tossed out the fruit. Kneeling again, I used it to bash and sever the spinal column. We both looked at the dead vampire, a mess in the once-immaculate house. Carlos moaned, taking our attention from the creature. Thank god Carlos was still alive.

"Last Christmas" began to play again. I looked at Henry's blood-splattered face. The pull of his brown eyes something I could no longer deny. Without question I kissed his lips, ignoring the taste of blood because his sweetness and my desire were so much more delicious. Like that first lick of candy cane.

"I suppose the devil made you do that?" His eyes twinkled like the star The Three Kings were destined to see. Everything happens for a reason. I wiped away the blood from his face the way I would tears. His expression of joy turned somber.

"We need to get back to my house. There were three coffins."

"Two more of them, you think?"

Carlos groaned as he sat up, covered in small cuts from the broken decorations, "What are we waiting for? I have a shotgun and a night vision headset in my Mustang. Can't have vampires being nesio during the holidays. Why couldn't they be like those sparkly ones my daughter used to love? Dios."

I looked around at what we could use to arm ourselves. We still had the roses. The piñata stick and a shotgun. There had to be more.

"We need to prepare, then we head out in my truck. Rip the rose petals off and stick them in your pockets. Henry, there is an axe on the side of the house with a stack of firewood. Carlos, you have the shotgun."

"More garlic?"

I looked around. "That." Hanging on the wall was a large braid of garlic my auntie gave me as a gift.

Henry squeezed my hand. "Okay, I think we are ready."

≋ ≋ ≋

There didn't seem to be anything out of place when we pulled up to the property.

Henry let out a heavy sigh. "I can't believe I invested in a vampire nest."

My hand touched his thigh. "We will get them all. This is yours."

"We should walk around the perimeter of the house. See if anything sticks out," said Carlos, his night vision goggles on.

We grabbed our weapons of choice and got out of my truck.

"We stick together at all times. No wandering. Let's start with the right side of the house and make our way around to the front door." Despite getting thrown into a tree Carlos was as tough as an armadillo getting knocked onto the side of the road, still able to keep going.

We approached the house with caution, Carlos leading the way with his night vision. Henry and I kept an eye out for what could lurk behind us. We peeked inside the windows of the parlor. Nothing. When we made it to the back, Carlos stopped us. "Look!"

The large shrubs that had once covered the windows also covered something else at the back of the property. We all stared at a wooden cellar door leading from beneath the house. Dirt had been thrown in all directions. Dim light could be seen inside. "Holy shit. That has been there this whole time. I thought it was a unused flower bed. *That* was under there?"

Carlos lifted his night vision to his forehead and then grabbed both our arms. "I don't think we go in there. Expected."

Henry turned and led the way. "The front. Let's go."

At the door he fumbled the keys with shaky hands. I touched his waist. "Focus."

He took a deep breath and pushed the key in as quietly as possible. The inside didn't look disturbed. Henry guided us through the parlor and office. Not being stupid or in a horror film, I flipped on as many lights as I could. We knew these fuckers were here. They wouldn't get us in the dark.

From the top of the landing that led to the basement we could see a light already on. It was bright. "The preparation room. I turned it off when I left."

We each lifted our weapons. They were waiting for us.

The preparation room made me gasp. It was covered in blood and bits of ripped flesh. This was where the vampire stuffed the body in my laundry room. Henry's tidy workspace had been transformed to an abattoir. "They must be in the other room. That's where the door outside has to lead to." Carlos and I glanced at Henry. He gave us a short nod before moving to the next room. The light wasn't on, but there was a glow. A large hole had been busted through the wall that appeared too thick for any human to remove.

"Another room. No wonder everything was destroyed."

Carlos brought his shotgun to shooting height, preparing to blast anything that might emerge from the hole. I had the piñata stick positioned to fuck a vamp up real good. Henry was ready to swing his axe. "We have to kill these fuckers before they realize the other one is dead. And who knows who else they have killed tonight."

I walked with quiet steps towards the hole. Carlos and Henry followed my lead. As we got closer, there was more light coming from inside the broken wall. I could see candles in all states of melted life dotting the floor.

"Dios," whispered Carlos. All the items to create the puzzle we opened were piled in a corner, the paper, the wood, the paint. And the walls. That wasn't paint. Thick lashing of red coated the interior. Bones lay in different piles on the floor.

Henry pressed against my body. "Just my fucking luck."

I began to speak. "I know . . ."

A hiss came from the darkest corner. We all tightened our grip on our weapons. Whatever was there had to know we brought the bloody fight to them. "Show yourself. One of you is dead. Thought you might like to know. You might be vampires, but don't ever cross a bruja."

From the shadow emerged a creature which looked like the old woman painted on the box. She wore a rope necklace with small, cleaned, human skulls. They were too small to be from adults. "Diabla! Your death will be a blessing to world," shouted Carlos.

Another figure moved from the darkness. It was a woman who looked like a mirror version of the male vampire we'd killed at my home. She wore a silky red gown with dried blots of black I assumed was blood. Her elongated fingers were caked with it. The voice was deep and slow. "I know he is dead. I felt it the moment it happened. Are you ready to die? I have no use for you except to drain you dry and let my mother eat your flesh."

I stepped closer. "No chance, cabrona. Not at this time of year."

The small witch, Perchta, opened her mouth and cackled. Daggers of yellow and black teeth were joined by yarns of red saliva. Without hesitation I rushed towards her with the piñata stick. She shrieked as loud as the vampire who I could see leaping towards Henry. Three shots fired next to me. Carlos cried out. More screams from both creatures that threatened to burst my eardrums as the sound echoed like hell's cymbals. All I wanted was to see my mother again and make love to Henry on Christmas, and as long as possible after that.

I continued to stab the haggard figure as black liquid sprayed my face and body. Her sharp talons on her feet and hands scratched at me. I ignored the pain as I had ignored every rejection and everyone who said I couldn't do it in my life. All the men who left and begged to come back thinking I would be up for second helpings of bullshit on a silver platter. All the closed doors with work I had to bang on until one opened. The finding of inner light to have hope, always. To comfort myself as a child and as an adult when no one else was around. No fucking thanks. Not in this life or the next.

Her chest convulsed with violence and I felt my body being pulled away by my hair. Henry and Carlos grabbed the vampire by her loose clothing. Half of her shoulder was gone from a shotgun shell blast. In my periphery I could see that Carlos had lost his gun. His face fucked up with a large scratch across the cheek. In her eyes, those black wells of whatever animated her, I could see the rage. The vampire we killed was the love of her life, the perfect fit. Her partner and lover for who knows how long. And in that rage was an even deeper sorrow and fear. Not feeling his warmth again even though their bodies might be cold. I had compassion for her, yet not enough to let her to destroy me or Henry. I took a handful of the rose petals from my pockets and shoved them in her face. She screamed and let me go. It was enough time for me to raise my piñata stick and Henry his axe. I pierced her heart and pressed until she fell back and stumbled over a pile of bones. As she thrashed on the floor, Henry severed her head. Carlos scrambled for his shotgun before putting it in the heaving mouth of Perchta and pulling the trigger.

Then a silence descended in the basement. The vibration of something evil breathing in and out of the room was gone.

I couldn't speak. Tears streamed from eyes seeing these creatures. As my mother would probably have done, I kneeled next to them. Instead of the cross I lifted my hands.

"Ancestors. Spirit. Cleanse this place. Release whatever dark energy lives in these beings. I breathed in and out, taking in the scent of the candles, thinking of the love I had with my mother, the lovemaking with Henry. I allowed those beautiful emotions to fill my body and hopefully expand into this dark place. I could feel Henry next to me. His arm wrapped around my shoulders. I knew I was not alone in this as he kissed my neck and cheek. I chuckled, "Not a bit of mistletoe around."

He kissed me again, harder, on the lips. "How about I promise you mistletoe on Christmas Eve? In bed all night and all Christmas day."

I smiled knowing my La Posada wish had come true, even if it wasn't in the Hallmark or Disney way I'd imagined. "It's a date."

Carlos cleared his throat. "Guys, I know I almost died twice tonight, but I'm still here. And from what I have seen, you are past dating. This is the real thing. Take it from an old man."

Henry and I laughed before gazing into each other's eyes again. "Feliz Navidad," I whispered.

"Merry Christmas," he whispered back.

THE END

PANCHO CLAUS VS. KRAMPUS

V. CASTRO

Dedicated to La Raza.
Your stories matter.

PANCHO CLAUS
VS.
KRAMPUS

Ribbons of green streaked across the sky as he felt his life slipping away. The light moved like ghoulish eels swimming in shallow water. What a beautiful sight. He always thought the final image before death would be the faces of his wife and daughter.

His body ached for their warmth and comfort. Blood leaked from the corner of his mouth that felt numb from the creature's blows as he shivered from the snow encasing his body. If his injuries didn't end him, then the frost would. Cholo's wet tongue licked his forehead that throbbed, but not nearly as much as whatever organs hemorrhaged inside of him. The green haze of the light appeared to get closer and closer as his eyes could no longer remain open.

***

Pancho couldn't remember the last time he went on a vacation. He consistently took time off between Christmas and New Year to spend time with the family, but afterwards it was back to arranging the logistics for the following Christmas with more children to visit. So many children in need. That is the legacy of Pancho Claus. A rebel with a cause in a sombrero and boots. Some impersonators liked to don a Zoot suit, but that wasn't his style. Their cause meant providing for those who deserved a little boost, a glimmer of hope and kindness. These are the small torches that stay with people on their darkest days to keep them going. Christmas spirit. It begins in childhood.

Being born into the clan was the gift he had grown to love, even though as a young man he had thought of it as a burden. His daughter Teresa took pride in their family legacy. She loved every second of taking command of the Christmas business. She was good at it, too. She returned from her Executive MBA program at Yale, excited by the idea of reaching even more children across the globe. Her plans beyond one day of the year. Real change. Pancho decided to see the Northern lights in Iceland, a dream he had always possessed but had never taken the time to venture beyond north of the

Texas border. Since completing his last Christmas, this dream would be a reality. His work only took him south of the equator, a pact made long ago between the Claus clans. Nicholas handled north and Pancho in charge of the south. Creating a special night for the children of the entire world was too big a task for a single person. Yes, there are auroras in the south pole, however, Nicholas promised an adventure in his new retirement residence, Iceland. Their wives enjoyed the warm waters of the Blue Lagoon near Reykjavik before joining their husbands for whale watching. Pancho couldn't wait to dip his aching muscles in the hot springs across the country. Nic had told him there was one spot in particular you must strip to your skin out in the open. Imagine that.

"Pop, stop fussing and go!" said his daughter Teresa.

"I know, mija, but I'm old and it's tough to see you running things. So confident, like your mother. Letting go is not easy. I will officially be retired soon."

"Mom had no problem flying out early. Now you and Cholo have fun in the wild. Enjoy your life."

"I will." Pancho gave his daughter a kiss on the forehead.

"Pop … Your phone and watch. I set up an Instagram account so you can show everyone your adventures."

Pancho rolled his eyes and took the new electronics off the kitchen counter before heading to the stables. "I will do my best. Love you."

The sun blazed that morning despite the winter chill. He wondered how he would cope with the Icelandic snow if he bristled at the Texas wind.

Pancho rushed into the warmth of the stables. Cholo, Pancho's best friend and trusted sidekick, would enjoy the wilderness. His glowing red eyes made him look like a thing from hell, and indeed he was built like a hellhound, standing nearly five feet tall, however, the two had been together since Pancho first took on this gig. When still just a small burro, Pancho allowed Cholo to sleep on the floor at the foot of their bed. As a child, Teresa sometimes dressed him up and fed him at the table like a doll. He was family.

"Are you ready, my friend? We are going on vacation!"

Cholo snorted and reared his head.

"I know. I know. But we are supposed to do retirement things. C'mon, we have a fancy private plane to catch to Iceland to meet Old St, Nic. I hear they made extra room for you."

***

"Nic, it's great to see you, man. How are you doing?" Pancho sat next to the bed of his dear friend hoping he would recover soon.

"Not great. This bronchitis has me bedridden. I'm sorry I can't join you. It is a clear night, too. Perfect to see the northern lights."

"You just tell me where to go. Me and Cholo got it covered. How are you liking your new home in Iceland?"

"I miss Norway, but this is a new phase in our lives. Closer to come bother you in the heat. As you know, Nicola is the boss now." Nic let out sneeze and cleared his throat of mucus before taking a sip of his steaming tea.

"I am pleased to hear you are adjusting. We will catch up later. Just feel better, old man."

"Who are you calling old man? Wait until I take you glacier climbing! I need to warn you. There has been talk of something wandering around the country. A tour guide found dozens of puffins

73

ripped to pieces. That's how I got this blasted infection. I gathered a few people, and we scouted the forests and caves for hours. Nothing."

Pancho didn't know much about the wildlife in Iceland, but if it was Texas it could just be a coyote or some other predator. He didn't want to press because Nic looked exhausted with his bloodshot eyes sagging. Hair grayer than he remembered, but he always had hair so blond it appeared white.

"Be well, my friend. I will keep alert."

Pancho left his friend with a sense of sadness. They were once so young and full of bullish life, comparing how fast they delivered gifts over shots of tequila chased with Modelo beer and shouting, "Skol!" He had to accept this retirement, old age, and take it easy. Old age sneaks up on you like a camouflaged diamondback in the desert. Bam! You are bit with loose skin and bedtime creeping earlier and earlier.

Nic's daughter, Nicola, stood by the door. "My father wanted me to give this to you before he left. It's a hunting knife from back home. We are told it has been handed down from the very first of our clan to help ward off the evil that would see all the generosity in the world taken away. As every year passes, it feels the generosity and goodwill crumble like icebergs in warming oceans."

Pancho looked at the long knife with a curved tip and whale bone handle decorated with various saints and runes. "I cannot accept this. It is a family heirloom."

Nicola curled her hand around the handle of the blade. "You can return it when you meet him again. It's a bit of peace of mind while out there."

"Thank you dear. And good luck with the new position."

Nicola smiled. "You mean as head of the clan or as your soon to be daughter in law?"

Pancho wrapped his arms around her in a bear hug, his eyes welling up. "I know you and Teresa will do wonderful things for the children of the world. You have made my daughter very happy."

"Thanks, Dad." Nicola kissed Pancho on the cheek. "Be careful. I have never seen the crew as worried as they were after the dead puffins. Before that, a carcass of a whale found torn to pieces."

"I will; it's probably nothing." Pancho climbed into his thick 66° North coat and boots.

"Pancho, there are no large predators here."

He looked at Nicola. A worm of fear wriggled in and out of his heart. His gaze shifted to the blade he had initially put down to leave. Instead he placed it into his coat's inner pocket. "I promise to be careful."

* * *

Cholo pulled the sled across the snow with glee, his glowing red eyes sparkling and his snorts creating puffs of white through the light snowfall. The burro enjoyed this change of scenery. The cold wind against Pancho's face as he glided across the snow filled him with an exhilaration he had not felt since Teresa arrived into the world. Perhaps retirement could be fun. So many new hobbies and experiences. He had spent his life giving to others, and now he could give a little for himself.

"Okay, boy. You can stop now." Pancho lifted his goggles and brought the smartphone closer to his face to check the GPS. This should be the right place. He looked up. The magnificent colors were just beginning to brighten the sky. The sound of breaking branches and crunching snow broke his wandering mind. He turned towards the noise. A bull's snort. Heavy breathing cast plumes of frozen air over the face of something fearsome. Its hair hung off its body like a tangled blanket, and even from this distance Pancho could smell the dried feces and urine upon its legs. Eyes that had no light or soul stared back, reflecting the glow of the lights in the sky. A stuttering guttural growl was the only sound in the forest. He had heard of this creature. It was a beast that devoured misbehaved children, like La Lechuza. "I don't want trouble, hombre, just leave us alone." Pancho could barely believe his eyes. Usually people didn't believe in him. He looked at Cholo, who was tied to the sled. Pancho took slow steps to release his friend.

"Trespasser," the creature screeched.

"Hey, I'm on vacation, and there was no sign. Nicolas invited me. You better be on your way."

"I will eat your heart and dry your pet's meat. Time to bring the world to black as night. All the children to feed our bellies and souls. This world deserves nothing less for all its wickedness. The time of judgment is upon you all." It let out a hideous laughter so cold, Pancho could feel the hypothermia settling into his bones and drowning his lungs with glacier water. Both of the creature's hands flexed and widened, its elongated nails on full show. It grabbed a chain slung over its shoulder and began to wind it in the air like a lasso. Pancho had been to many rodeos in his youth, he knew this routine. He had also learned to be quick on his feet because his wife loved to dance. She taught him to cumbia and salsa, even dragged him to the occasional Honky Tonk. Truth be known, he preferred rock 'n roll. Ain't no party without good hairband music. Pancho glanced at his burro. The very sound of the chain cutting through the air made him feel dizzy.

Cholo's eyes always glowed red, but tonight they burned with volcanic magma, the power of the great Popocatepetl in Mexico. It seemed they would need all the help they could get. This thing wanted blood. Cholo cried out and scraped his hooves in the snow. With all his strength, he bounded towards the creature. Cholo drove the beast across the snow. Krampus backhanded Cholo against a snow drift. His body sunk and hind legs struggled to move against the weight of snow and ice.

"Cholo!" Pancho screamed. Now Pancho wanted blood. The blade. He remembered the blade in his coat as he dodged and weaved the chain like a Luchador. To survive, he would have to be swift as one. The two circled each other in the snow. Cholo cried into the night. Pancho squinted his eyes in the darkness. He thanked all the saints he took his wife Melanie's advice and had the eye surgery. Krampus gave the chain another swing and tossed it towards Pancho. Before he could move out of the way, it struck one of his ankles. Pancho screamed in pain as the bone crunched and fire sprinted up the length of his leg. Krampus took the opportunity to drive into Pancho the same way Cholo did to it. One blow struck Pancho across the face, then the chest; all of his oxygen fled like a snow angel above his head. The beast's mouth opened wide, revealing jagged teeth and a pointed tongue coated with a white paste. Its viscous drool, smelling of decay, covered Pancho's face.

"Are you ready to be the first sacrifice?"

Pancho turned his head towards Cholo. He only wanted his best friend to get away from this thing. Cholo was gone. Pancho managed a smile before bringing the blade, still in his hand, into the beast's ribs and pulling it out again. Let it bleed out. As Krampus yelled at the sudden jolt of pain, Cholo shot from the side, knocking Krampus off Pancho. Krampus writhed on the ground from the oozing wound. As the creature jerked upright, Cholo kicked his hind legs into Krampus's skull. Pancho winced and yelled out in pain as he attempted to lift himself up. He placed one hand over his chest that felt crushed, his breathing labored and painful. He had to see if it was still alive. Cholo pushed him the best he could with his head as Pancho dragged himself across the snow until he was close enough to see with his own eyes. A horn dangled off the creature's scalp by a thin layer of flesh, exposing shattered bone and brain matter. Both eyes caved in with seeping black jelly leaking from the corners. That horrible tongue hung lifeless at the corner of the mouth. Good. Something like that should not exist. There was enough hate and chaos in the world. Too many children already devoured by abuse or poverty. Some left to die in cages in his own home state, an evil he had thought he would never see. There was no need for this creature. Pancho swayed as he grabbed his throbbing ribs. The sweat from the fight now dried on his skin, allowing the cold to seep into his bones. Without any control over his body, Pancho fell to the snow. Cholo licked his friend, nuzzled his neck. He could sense Pancho's heart was slowing. With his teeth, he grabbed Pancho by the collar of his blood-soaked coat. He was heavy, far too heavy to drag to safety. As Cholo continued to pull, the phone fell out of the pocket of Pancho's snow pants. It buzzed. Cholo pressed the blinking red button with his nose.

"Papa? Where are you? Hello? Your watch alerted me to your heart rate."

Cholo recognized the voice as Teresa. He let out a cry. With all the sadness and fear, he hoped Teresa would understand. Teresa spoke again but not to Cholo. The phone went black. No light except the green eels swimming in the atmosphere.

***

"Who is the bedridden old man now!" Pancho opened his eyes. He couldn't have asked for a better sight. Nic peered into his face looking ruddy and healthy, his voice booming. Teresa, Melanie, Nicola, and Cholo surrounded him.

"I thought I was a dead man. What happened?" "Pop, that watch I gave you for Christmas also tracks your vitals. Mom suggested it after seeing you scoff chili con queso and chips almost every night. She was worried about your cholesterol. Anyway, I called Nicola, and she arranged an emergency helicopter to find you. Watch also has GPS."

"But I wouldn't be here without my wonderful Cholo. Burro of the year. He gets all the treats."

Nic leaned in close. "We saw the thing. Krampus. Not sure how it got to Iceland, but it is usually only in Europe, which tells me they are on the move."

81

"What? There are more of them? I mean, it did say judgment was coming. I was too concerned about surviving to think about what it was saying."

"I've contacted friends across Europe. We should know more soon."

Teresa nodded and reached for her father's hand. "It's no longer just about caring for the children. We have another mission, and that is to find the rest of those beasts before they cause chaos."

Pancho wished it had been all a bad dream, but he knew it wasn't. "I'm ready. Retirement sounded boring anyway."

THE END

ACKNOWLEDGEMENTS

I would like to acknowledge Platform House for their fantastic formatting and book services.

Grim Poppy for cover design for this novelette and Dia de Los Slashers.

About the Author

V.Castro is a two time Bram Stoker Award nominated Mexican American writer from San Antonio, Texas now residing in the UK. She writes horror, erotic horror, and science fiction.

Her books include *The Haunting of Alejandra, Alien: Vasquez, Mestiza Blood, The Queen of the Cicadas, Out of Aztlan, Las Posadas,* and *Goddess of Filth.*

Her forthcoming novel is *Immortal Pleasures from Del Rey.*

Connect with Violet:

Instagram@vlatinalondon

Twitter@vlatinalondon

www.vcastrostories.com

TikTok@vcastrobooks

Goodreads

Amazon

She can also be found on Blue Sky.

Printed in Great Britain
by Amazon

33404649R00050